The School Trip

by Geoff Patton
illustrated by David Clarke

RISING★STARS

to Sam's
house

the
school

the
supermarket

2

to Con's hou

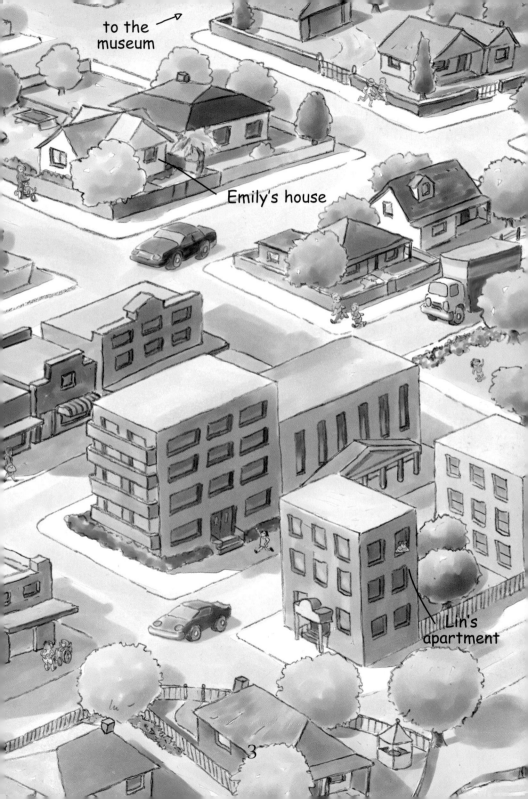

me
(Emily)

Franco   Mico

4

Hi. My name is Emily.
This is a picture of my class.

Chapter 1
Line up

Today we are going to the
Museum. Ms Hinkle says,
'Everyone line up.'

'Line up,' says Franco.
'Line up,' says Mico.
'Line up,' says Chico.

We all line up. Well, everyone *except*
Franco, Mico and Chico.
Ms Hinkle says our line looks more
like a snake than a line.

Franco hisses like a snake.
So does Mico. So does Chico.
'Boys are *so* immature,' I say
to Ms Hinkle.

Ms Hinkle says nothing,
but I think I see her smile.

Chapter 2
On the Bus

'Everyone sit down in
a seat,' says Ms Hinkle.

'Sit down,' says Franco.
'Sit down,' says Mico.
'Sit down,' says Chico.

We all sit in our seats. Well, everyone *except* Franco, Mico and Chico. They say they are busting. They say they *have* to go to the toilet.

'You should have gone *before* we got on the bus,' says Ms Hinkle.

Franco crosses his legs.
So does Mico. So does Chico.
I say, 'Boys are *so* immature.'

Ms Hinkle says nothing,
but I think I hear her sigh.

Chapter 3
Singing along

On the way to the museum,
Ms Hinkle says, 'Let's sing a song.'

'Let's sing a song,' says Franco.
'Let's sing a song,' says Mico.
'Let's sing a song,' says Chico.

We all sing a song. Well, everyone
except Franco, Mico and Chico.
They play the drums with their
hands on the back of the seat.

'Singing only,' says Ms Hinkle.

Franco sings at the top of his voice.
So does Mico. So Does Chico.
They think they are rock stars.
I say, 'Boys are *so* immature.'

Ms Hinkle says nothing,
but I think I see her frown.

Chapter 4
The Museum

At the museum Ms Hinkle says,
'Please do not touch anything.'

'Don't touch,' says Franco
'Don't touch,' says Mico
'Don't touch,' says Chico.

No-one touches anything.
Well, no-one *except*
Franco, Mico and Chico.
They say they have found
some bones.

'Where did you find them?'
says Ms Hinkle.

I think I know where they
found them ... in the skeleton
of the Tyrannosaurus Rex!
'Boys are *so* immature,' I say
to Ms Hinkle.

Boys are *so* immature.

Ms Hinkle says nothing,
but I think I see her glare.

Chapter 5
Hanging Out on Mars

We go into the Space Dome.
Ms Hinkle says, 'Everyone
hold hands.'

'Hold hands,' says Franco.
'Hold hands,' says Mico.
'Hold hands,' says Chico.

We all hold hands. Well, everyone *except* Franco, Mico and Chico. They say they are *too big* to hold hands.

Franco goes missing.
So does Mico. So does Chico.
'Where are those boys?' says Ms Hinkle.

We find them hanging
from Mars.
'Boys are *so* immature,'
I say to Ms Hinkle.

Boys are *so*
immature.

Ms Hinkle says nothing,
but I think I see her cry.

Chapter 6
Home Again

'Time to go back to school,' says
Ms Hinkle. 'Let's all have a sleep
on the bus,' she says.
'Let's sleep,' says Franco. 'Let's sleep,'
says Mico. 'Let's sleep,' says Chico.
And they do.

Boys are not *immature*,' I say to
Ms Hinkle, 'when they are asleep.'
Ms Hinkle says nothing,
but I know I see her smile.

Survival Tips

Tips for surviving an excursion

1. Make sure you have fun – even if the trip is somewhere you don't want to go.

2. Ignore Franco, Mico and Chico.

3. Don't eat too much on the bus – being sick on the bus is no fun, especially in front of your friends.

4. Ignore Franco, Mico and Chico.

5 Line up at the front so you get the best seat on the bus.

6 Ignore Franco, Mico and Chico.

7 Take ear plugs in case the singing on the bus gets too bad.

8 Always go to the toilet before you get on the bus – even if you don't want to go.

9 Ignore Franco, Mico and Chico.

Riddles and Jokes

Mico	What do dinosaurs put on their fries?
Chico	Tomatosaurus
Ms Hinkle	What do you call a dinosaur wearing high heels?
Emily	My-feet-o-saurus.
Ms Hinkle	Franco, I hope I didn't see you copying from Emily's maths test.
Franco	I hope you didn't see me either!
Ms Hinkle	What family does the Tyrannosaurus Rex belong to?
Chico	Nobody's family I know.
Ms Hinkle	How did Mico fall on the floor?
Emily	He tripped on the cordless phone.